This book
belongs to

For all key workers.
Your tireless work has been
an inspiration to us all.

With thanks to Inclusive Minds for connecting us with

their Inclusion Ambassador network and in particular

to Hannah Hoskins for her input.

Published by
PEACHTREE PUBLISHING COMPANY INC.
1700 Chattahoochee Avenue
Atlanta, Georgia 30318-2112
PeachtreeBooks.com

First published in Great Britain in 2021 by Two Hoots, an imprint of Pan Macmillan
First United States version published in 2022 by Peachtree Publishing Company Inc.

The illustrations were rendered in gouache and digital.

Printed in January 2022 in China
10 9 8 7 6 5 4 3 2 1
First Edition

ISBN: 978-1-68263-456-1

Cataloging-in-Publication Data is available from the Library of Congress

THREE
LITTLE VIKINGS

Bethan Woollvin

PEACHTREE

ATLANTA

Deep in the forest, the Viking folk were celebrating their latest haul of treasure.

All except best friends Ebba, Helga, and Wren. They were playing when they heard a strange noise outside.

"Chieftain," Helga said, "there's something scary outside!"

"Nonsense!" the Chieftain replied. "I know that is just a thunderstorm . . . and I know best!"

Later that night, the three girls were tucked up in bed reading spooky stories. They huddled together while the rumbling and crashing continued outside.

"Do you think it's really just a storm?" Wren whispered.

Eventually the ruckus stopped, and the girls drifted off to sleep.

The next morning, Helga, Ebba, and Wren woke to find their village in chaos.

"It looks like something very BIG was here," Helga said, suspiciously.

"Nonsense!" said the Chieftain. "I know it was just a fox . . . and I know best!"

So the girls went about their day, playing until dark. As they left for home, a loud roaring erupted from the forest and trees tumbled to the ground right before them.

"What was that?" Helga asked, nervously.

"I'm not sure," Wren said, "but it sounds like something angry!"

Dashing back to the village, the girls hurried
to find the Chieftain.

"A BIG, angry, noisy creature is roaming the
forest, destroying the trees!" Ebba told him.

"Nonsense," boomed the Chieftain. "I know the trees

are just rotten . . . and I know best!"

"But it's REALLY big!" Ebba said, louder.

"Stop bothering me! The village treasure has gone missing,

and I must find out who is behind it."

"It was probably the same creature who knocked down all the trees!" Ebba said.

"Nonsense!" the Chieftain shouted. "I know it was just some pesky ravens . . . and I know best!"

The Chieftain *said* he knew best, but the girls hadn't seen a storm, or a fox, or a rotten tree, or any thieving ravens. So they decided to investigate for themselves.

"I think we need to go
back to the woods,"
Ebba said.

Helga, Ebba, and Wren followed
a set of footprints into the forest,
but they led to . . . nothing.

"We might find a clue in my book
about spooky creatures!" Ebba said.

The little Vikings nestled onto
a tree branch and checked Ebba's
book for answers.

"What about this one?" Wren asked.

"It only comes out at night . . .

it leaves a trail of destruction . . .

it loves shiny things . . ."

"IT'S A TROLL!"

Safely back in the village, Helga, Ebba, and Wren wasted no time at all in finding the Chieftain.

"THERE'S A TROLL ON THE LOOSE!" they yelled. "We saw him in the forest!"

"Nonsense!" replied the Chieftain. "I know trolls do not exist . . . and I know best!"

But the little Vikings had an inkling that Ebba's book knew better . . . and so they hatched a plan to defeat the troll themselves.

Carrying a shiny pot of gold, Helga, Ebba, and Wren walked deep into the forest until they heard a familiar bashing and smashing.

"Hey you!" shouted Wren.

Sure enough, the troll couldn't resist the treasure.

The horrid troll growled and chased after
the little Vikings, until . . .

he saw something even shinier
than their pot of gold.

It was the
Chieftain's armor!

"HELP! It's a
TROLL!"

he shouted.

The troll chased the Chieftain up
a mountain and straight into . . .

the dawning sun! As golden rays fell on
the troll, he transformed into wood, his
roots burrowing deep into the ground.

"Got him!" cheered the little Vikings.

That night, the village gathered before an *unusually* large fire as the little Vikings shared the story of their triumphant victory.

"We beat the troll," the girls cheered,
"because *we* know best!"